SNOW WHITE
and the Seven Dwarfs

Text by Maureen Spurgeon

Brown Watson

ENGLAND

A MESSAGE TO PARENTS

It is of vital importance for parents to read good books to young children in order to aid the child's psychological and intellectual development. At the same time as stimulating the child's imagination and awareness of his environment, it creates a positive relationship between parent and child. The child will gradually increase his basic vocabulary and will soon be able to read books alone.

Brown Watson has published this series of books with these aims in mind. By collecting this inexpensive library, parent and child are provided with hours of pleasurable and profitable reading.

Long ago, a queen sat sewing at a palace window. Looking out at the white snow drifting against the black window frame, she pricked her finger and three drops of blood fell. "If only, I had a daughter with skin as white as snow, blood-red cheeks and hair as black as the window frame," she sighed, "I would call her Snow White."

Before long, the queen's wish was granted. Everyone celebrated the birth of her baby daughter. And, as the years passed, Snow White became more and more beautiful.

But the happy times were not to last. Suddenly, the good queen became ill and died. Within a year, Snow White's father had taken another wife, as hard-hearted as she was beautiful.

The new queen was also very vain. Her greatest treasure was a magic mirror, and every day she asked it the same question. "Mirror, mirror on the wall, who is the fairest one of all?"

The answer from the magic
mirror was always the same.
"In all the land,
'Tis thou, oh queen!
Thou art the fairest
To be seen!"

Then, one day, the mirror gave
a different answer.
"No maiden was more fair
Than thou!
But Snow White is
The fairest, now!"

The queen flew into a terrible
rage, screaming for a palace
guard.
"Take Snow White into the forest!"
she stormed. "Put her to death!
Then bring me back her heart!"

The guard was shocked. He knew he had to do as the queen said. But, by the time he and Snow White reached the forest, he had made up his mind that he could never do such a wicked deed.

He told her of the danger she was in. "Run away, as far as you can," he begged Snow White, "so the queen will not find you! I shall take back a deer's heart and pretend it is your's!"

Poor Snow White! She would never have thought anyone could hate her so much. On and on she ran, strange shadows looming everywhere, and thorns

and brambles seeming to reach out, clawing at her. How long she kept running, she hardly knew. It seemed like a dream when, quite suddenly, she came across a little cottage nestling in the very heart of the forest.

"Anyone at home?" she called, stepping inside. How dusty and untidy it was in that little cottage! But Snow White was so glad to have somewhere to rest, she did not mind.

She set to work, feeling much
happier as she laid a fire, ready
to cook some broth.
"I wonder who lives here?" she
thought, dusting the seven little
chairs set around the table.

By the time she had washed seven little plates, seven mugs, seven knives, spoons and forks, then made seven little beds, Snow White was feeling very tired. She only meant to rest a little while . . .

When she woke up, there were the faces of the seven dwarfs smiling at her. How pleased they had been to return to a warm, clean cottage, and find a meal waiting for them, cooked by a pretty girl!

As soon as they heard what had happened to her, the dwarfs said she could stay with them. Snow White had not been so happy for a long time. She loved looking after the seven dwarfs.

"Do not open the door to anyone
while we are out," they told her.
"If ever the queen should hear
where you are, she will surely
try to harm you again." Snow
White knew this was true.

At that very moment, the magic
mirror was telling the queen,
"In the seven dwarfs' cottage,
Snow White lives now.
She is, dear queen,
Still fairer than thou!"

The queen went white with
rage! Determined to put an end
to Snow White, she disguised
herself as an old pedlar woman,
then put poison into the rosiest
apple she could find . . .

With her magic powers, the queen soon found the cottage in the forest and tapped at the door. "Lovely apples!" she croaked, as Snow White came to the window. "Try one, my dear."

Snow White did not want to hurt an old woman's feelings. One bite of the poisoned apple and she fell to the floor. Cackles of wild laughter from the wicked queen echoed all through the forest.

The dwarfs were heartbroken when they found dear Snow White. Wanting to keep her with them for always, they put her in a crystal casket and set it down in her favourite part of the forest.

The moment he saw Snow White, he had to lean over and kiss her. Her eyelids fluttered, and as she looked into the face of the young prince, she knew she loved him as much as he already loved her.

As time passed, the story of the beautiful young princess asleep in a crystal casket began to spread. One day, a handsome young prince decided to discover the truth for himself.